ADVENTURES IN MATH

HOW TO **LEVEL UP** YOUR **MATH GAME**

Written by **CARLEIGH WU**

Illustrated by **SEAN SIMPSON**

Kids Can Press

Text © 2025 Carleigh Wu
Illustrations © 2025 Sean Simpson

All rights reserved. No part of this publication may be reproduced, stored in a retrieval system or transmitted, in any form or by any means, without the prior written permission of Kids Can Press Ltd. or, in case of photocopying or other reprographic copying, a license from The Canadian Copyright Licensing Agency (Access Copyright). For an Access Copyright license, visit www.accesscopyright.ca or call toll free to 1-800-893-5777.

Many of the designations used by manufacturers and sellers to distinguish their products are claimed as trademarks. Where those designations appear in this book and Kids Can Press Ltd. was aware of a trademark claim, the designations have been printed in initial capital letters (e.g., Rubik's Cube).

Published in Canada and the U.S. by Kids Can Press Ltd.
25 Dockside Drive, Toronto, ON M5A 0B5

Kids Can Press is a Corus Entertainment Inc. company

www.kidscanpress.com

The artwork in this book was created with pencil, paper and digital tools.
The text is set in Gargle, Open Sans and Rock Bro.

Edited by Patricia Ocampo
Designed by Andrew Dupuis

Printed and bound in Shenzhen, China, in 3/2025 by C & C Offset

CM 25 0 9 8 7 6 5 4 3 2 1

LIBRARY AND ARCHIVES CANADA CATALOGUING IN PUBLICATION

Title: Adventures in math: how to level up your math game / written by Carleigh Wu; illustrated by Sean Simpson.
Names: Wu, Carleigh, author. | Simpson, Sean, illustrator.
Description: Includes bibliographical references and index.
Identifiers: Canadiana (print) 20240525426 | Canadiana (ebook) 20250102382 | ISBN 9781525311321 (hardcover) | ISBN 9781525313080 (EPUB)
Subjects: LCSH: Mathematics — Juvenile literature.
Classification: LCC QA40.5 .W8 2025 | DDC j510 — dc23

Kids Can Press gratefully acknowledges that the land on which our office is located is the traditional territory of many nations, including the Mississaugas of the Credit, the Anishnabeg, the Chippewa, the Haudenosaunee and the Wendat Peoples, and is now home to many diverse First Nations, Inuit and Métis Peoples.

We thank the Government of Ontario, through Ontario Creates and the Ontario Arts Council; the Canada Council for the Arts; and the Government of Canada for their financial support of our publishing activity.

TABLE OF **CONTENTS**

① INTO THE JUNGLE — 7
② BETTER TOGETHER — 21
③ HELPFUL MISTAKES — 31
④ CREATE IT! — 43
⑤ BULLET HOLES AND PIE CHARTS — 57

IT ALL ADDS UP — 71

ACKNOWLEDGMENTS — 73

AUTHOR'S SELECTED SOURCES — 74

INDEX — 78

"Mathematics is not about numbers,
equations, computations or algorithms:
it is about understanding."

William Paul Thurston,
American mathematician

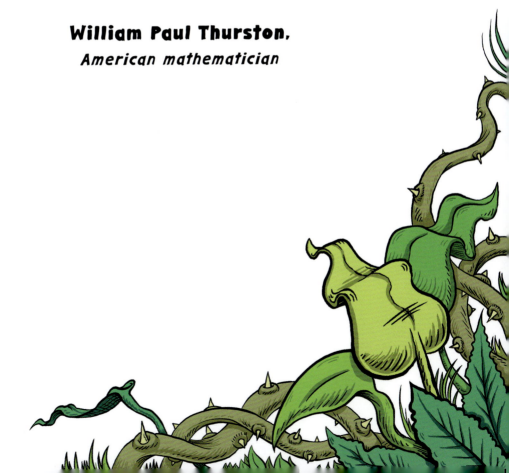

INTO THE JUNGLE

Imagine you're an explorer trying to find your way out of the jungle.

You start walking in one direction. The vines are too dense — it's a dead end. You turn back.

You find another path, but it's steep. You zigzag your way up, back and forth, slow and steady. You keep going, hoping that at the top you'll see the path out. But when you finally reach the top, a thick fog descends. You continue walking. Are you making any progress at all? Haven't you passed by that same rock before?

Suddenly, the fog lifts. At that moment, you see what you couldn't see before. "Eureka!" You break into a run along the path. Could it be possible that you've found the way out? You push on.

Math is hard. It takes time. You might feel frustrated. But it's also an adventure. And when you find the solution, you'll be excited and feel a sense of accomplishment.

Welcome to the jungle!

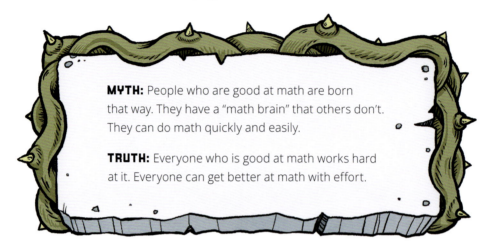

MYTH: People who are good at math are born that way. They have a "math brain" that others don't. They can do math quickly and easily.

TRUTH: Everyone who is good at math works hard at it. Everyone can get better at math with effort.

Math myths are harmful in a sneaky sort of way. They suggest that some people are "math people" and others are not and nothing can be changed about it. Worse, you don't even know you're affected by these rigid beliefs.

Throughout this book, we'll look at different math myths. To help debunk them, you'll read about people who have used math to do amazing things. Their stories will help change how you think about math — and your ability to do it well.

MARYAM MIRZAKHANI
Born: May 12, 1977, Iran

"It is like being lost in a jungle and trying to use all the knowledge that you can gather to come up with some new tricks, and with some luck you might find a way out."

In sixth grade, Maryam Mirzakhani didn't think she was very good in math ... and neither did her teacher! When her teacher handed back the marked final tests for the class, Maryam shredded hers and put the scraps in her backpack. She told her best friend, Roya, she wasn't going to try to do better at math.

The next year, Maryam had a different teacher, who was more encouraging. Maryam and Roya enjoyed math so much that they wanted spots on Iran's Math Olympiad team, which competed against different countries. The two friends were determined to go, even though Iran had never had girls on their team before.

Maryam and Roya found copies of old tests and tried them. It took them days to answer half the questions. (In the real test, they'd have only hours.) Still, they knew they could do it, if only they had the right instruction. They asked their principal for help.

Their school created a course for them, like the boys had, on how to answer the Olympiad questions. The girls earned places on the team and returned home with medals. Roya won silver; Maryam won gold.

Maryam and Roya went on to have successful careers in mathematics, teaching and researching at prestigious universities.

Maryam was the first Iranian and the first woman to win the Fields Medal, one of the highest honors a mathematician can receive. To keep learning, Maryam worked slowly and deeply. She asked lots of questions. She persevered.

Although Maryam died from cancer in 2017, she continues to inspire people. There is an annual math award called the Maryam Mirzakhani New Frontiers Prize for female mathematicians.

Effort Is Everything

In her book *Mindset*, psychologist Carol Dweck described two mindsets: fixed and growth. A fixed mindset is a belief that we are born with set abilities and talent and can't do much to change them. A growth mindset is a belief that through effort and perseverance we can get better.

A growth mindset means that when you learn something new and don't quite understand it, you say to yourself, "I don't understand *yet*." This gives you the confidence to work on it, to trust that it will get easier, even though it's hard right now. Words are important. As Carol said, the word *yet* can be very powerful. Students who believed intelligence can change did better on all three areas (reading, science and math) of an international test administered by the Organisation for Economic Cooperation and Development.

How can we develop a growth mindset? One way is through stories. In one study, researchers had two groups of students read stories about mathematicians. The difference was the message in the stories. One group of students read about the natural genius of mathematicians and their great achievements. Afterward, these students didn't think they could improve their math abilities. They felt they either knew their stuff or didn't. They had adopted a fixed mindset.

The other group of students read stories about the persistence and hard work behind mathematicians' great discoveries. These students adopted a growth mindset. They persevered and spent more time understanding math problems. The different *messages* of the stories led the students to approach math in different ways.

What stories do you tell yourself about what you can or can't do?

MIND OVER MATH

Use the Goldilocks Rule

In math class, if something feels too challenging and you don't understand, it's important to ask for help. Math ideas build on each other. Think of learning math like climbing a ladder. You can't reach the top rung without using the lower rungs. If you build your knowledge one rung at a time, you will feel secure as you advance to the top.

You need to use the Goldilocks Rule. That's where the math isn't too hard *or* too easy — it's just right. Tutors, teachers and online support can help. James Clear, author of the book *Atomic Habits*, wrote that the Goldilocks Rule helps you stay motivated. He recommended that you also "measure your progress and receive immediate feedback whenever possible."

You don't need to do Math Olympiad–level problems at the beginning. Even Maryam and Roya, who eventually won medals at those competitions, needed to practice and have special instruction on how to answer the questions. Remember, too, that even when math problems are just-right challenges, learning new ideas might take more time. Have confidence in your ability. Don't feel rushed to finish your math worksheet in class. You don't have to be the first person to solve a problem. The most important thing is to understand the concepts you're learning.

> Take your time as you work through math problems. The goal isn't to be quick but to understand.

JOHN MIGHTON
Born: October 2, 1957, Canada

"The myths surrounding the subject encourage children to give up the moment they encounter any difficulty."

When he was young, John Mighton read a book about mathematicians with superior minds — born geniuses. Since math didn't come as easily to him as it seemed to for those geniuses, John figured he wasn't born with a "math brain."

John worked hard to become a writer and eventually became a playwright. When his first major production was performed onstage, local reviewers slammed it. One critic called it a "muddled mess." Still, John kept writing. He knew that with practice and effort, he'd get better. And he did. His plays have won major awards and been performed in countries around the world.

John knew that writing well was something that could be learned. But for a long time, he didn't feel the same way about math. He believed, like many people, that you needed to be born with a math brain. Then he took a part-time job tutoring students in math. He needed the extra cash and the pay was steady, and he felt he could teach the basics well enough.

Some of the students had been diagnosed with learning disabilities. John broke each math skill into small steps, and the children began to excel. He became interested in how we learn. John also began to understand math more deeply through teaching others. He saw student after student grow from a math-hating kid into one who enjoyed it. He began to wonder: Could *I* excel in math?

John decided to put the same effort and persistence he had put into writing toward learning math. He went back to school to earn a math degree. He kept going until he earned his PhD (the highest level in school) in mathematics.

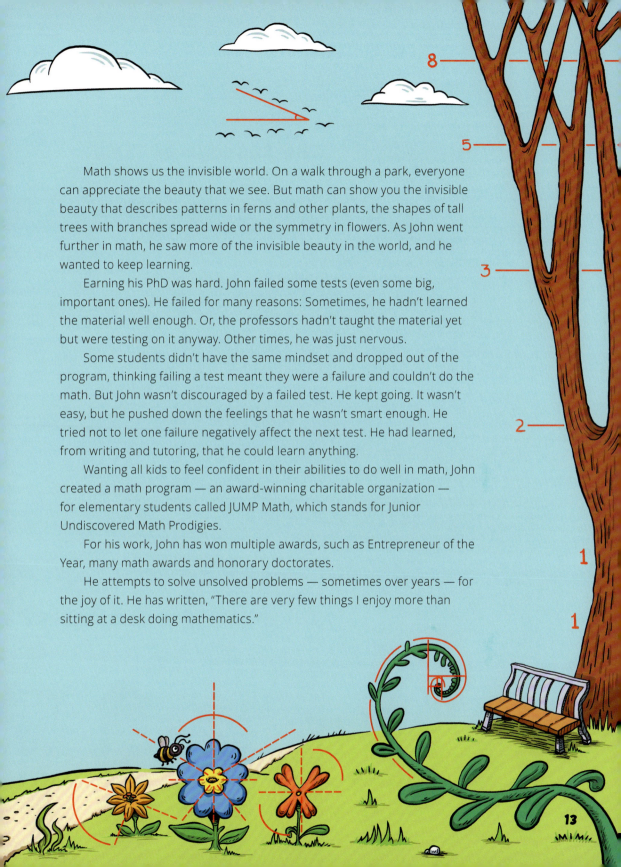

Math shows us the invisible world. On a walk through a park, everyone can appreciate the beauty that we see. But math can show you the invisible beauty that describes patterns in ferns and other plants, the shapes of tall trees with branches spread wide or the symmetry in flowers. As John went further in math, he saw more of the invisible beauty in the world, and he wanted to keep learning.

Earning his PhD was hard. John failed some tests (even some big, important ones). He failed for many reasons: Sometimes, he hadn't learned the material well enough. Or, the professors hadn't taught the material yet but were testing on it anyway. Other times, he was just nervous.

Some students didn't have the same mindset and dropped out of the program, thinking failing a test meant they were a failure and couldn't do the math. But John wasn't discouraged by a failed test. He kept going. It wasn't easy, but he pushed down the feelings that he wasn't smart enough. He tried not to let one failure negatively affect the next test. He had learned, from writing and tutoring, that he could learn anything.

Wanting all kids to feel confident in their abilities to do well in math, John created a math program — an award-winning charitable organization — for elementary students called JUMP Math, which stands for Junior Undiscovered Math Prodigies.

For his work, John has won multiple awards, such as Entrepreneur of the Year, many math awards and honorary doctorates.

He attempts to solve unsolved problems — sometimes over years — for the joy of it. He has written, "There are very few things I enjoy more than sitting at a desk doing mathematics."

HISTORY — The Passage of Time

For most of history, we hardly knew anything about how our world works, but we've always been curious about it. Mathematicians' curiosity pushed them to explore the mysteries of life, such as how to measure the passage of time.

The Babylonians of Mesopotamia (modern-day Iraq) created a system of counting using a base of 60, likely inherited from the Sumerian civilization. (One theory for this is that you can count to 60 using your two hands, if you use parts of the fingers — excluding the thumb — between joints.) We measure time using 60 minutes in an hour and 60 seconds in a minute. Around the world, different civilizations invented machines to tell time. The sundial, the water clock and the hourglass were eventually replaced by more modern machines, such as mechanical, electric and atomic clocks. Each new technology improved upon the last.

To create our calendar, civilizations built on the ideas of others. We know that it takes roughly 365 ¼ days for Earth to rotate around the sun. Wait a minute ... How do we count one-quarter of a day? The Romans decided that a year would be 365 days, rounding down, which we follow today. But every four years, we add an extra day in February to make that year have 366 days. This makes up for the four quarter days we missed — it's called a leap year.

Although we have learned a lot from explorers, scientists and mathematicians, there is a lot we still don't know. One day, we will discover new information that changes our understanding of the universe and ourselves.

HOW CAN THIS STORY HELP YOU WITH MATH?

Have you ever looked at the star-filled night sky? Or wondered why the moon looks different from night to night? When you look up, what do you notice? What do you wonder? In the stories in this chapter, you'll notice a common theme: mathematicians are curious. They wonder at the passage of time, the shape of Earth, the night sky and so much more. These questions can lead to wrong answers, but they can also push people to find correct ones.

In math class, stay curious. Ask yourself: Why is that answer correct? Is there another way to get the answer? Try to find more ways to solve a problem. Stay open to new possibilities.

Some people think they are born with set abilities. **THIS ISN'T TRUE.** You can change your abilities through effort and perseverance.

Learning New Things

Professor Dan Ariely has studied human behavior, including phenomena like motivation (why we do what we do). He has given the example of mountain climbers. After they finally get to the top, you'd expect them to say, "This was a terrible mistake. I'll never do it again." But they continue to go up again and again. Why? For them, the challenge and the struggle are both meaningful. But they also get to see the incredible views. You learn math for a similar reason — for the challenge and to see a view of the world that only math can show you.

Remember the times you tried to learn how to do something, like drawing or skating or playing an instrument? You weren't very good at the beginning, but you kept trying and it became easier and easier. You got better.

When you sit in math class, it's important to remember how much you have learned already. Think back a few years. Look at how far you've come. Things that once seemed challenging in math class are now easy, like counting to 100 or adding small numbers. You practiced until it got easier.

When we do hard things, like learning something new, or when we struggle through a math problem, we challenge ourselves. That struggle and the frustration and discomfort we feel are part of learning. They can show you what you don't know and can be a reminder that it's time to ask for help. When we eventually learn that new skill or solve that problem, we're going to feel great!

MULTIPLY YOUR POTENTIAL

Think Like an Explorer (Or a Filmmaker!)

Many mathematicians think of themselves as explorers, going places no one else has ever gone and learning new things about our world. This is how artistic people look at the world, too.

One of the first animators at Pixar, the Academy Award winner Andrew Stanton, compared creating a movie to sailing across the ocean. He said that when you sail, you don't try to avoid the weather. He explained, "You have to embrace that sailing means that you can't control the elements and that there will be good days and bad days and that, whatever comes, you will deal with it because your goal is to eventually get to the other side. You will not be able to control exactly how you get across." This is what it's like to create a movie — or do anything creative or new.

Doing math is creative and involves concentration and effort. Thinking of yourself as an explorer sailing the ocean can be helpful. It shows you that it won't be easy and there will be setbacks, but when you get to the other side, to the top or through it, you'll feel amazing because you'll see a new view of the world.

Imagining yourself persevering through something exciting but challenging — like sailing in rough seas — can push you through math problems.

SHOW YOUR WORK

In this book, you'll find a challenge at the end of every chapter. Writing and drawing will help you organize what you think. Reflecting on this chapter, complete one of the activities below:

1. Write about a time when something first seemed hard but then later seemed easy.
2. Write down some positive things to tell yourself when you face a challenge.
3. What did you learn from the stories of the mathematicians Maryam Mirzakhani and John Mighton?
4. Draw or write what it's like to explore undiscovered territory. Are you spelunking through an ice cave? Hiking through a dense forest? Sailing uncharted seas?

Peter M. Gollwitzer has been researching how we can make changes in our behavior. He's found interesting results with when/then statements. If you say, "**When** this happens, **then** I will do that," there is a big difference in your capacity to accomplish something. See page 63 for more details.

Look at this badge and remember:
When the voice in your head tells you, "I can't," **then** tell yourself, "I can't *yet* — but if I keep going, soon I'll be able to."

2
BETTER TOGETHER

You thought you'd found your way out of the jungle, but you're lost again. You need help. You have an idea, but will it work? What you need is a partner, someone you can talk to. Someone with binoculars. If only you could see just a little bit farther …

You're having trouble concentrating. You keep swatting at buzzing mosquitoes. They're everywhere! Too bad you don't have any bug spray in your pack.

Also, a granola bar would be nice. You're famished!

Luckily, you're not alone. You have a team!

You turn to your team and say, "I've got an idea. Do you see any problems with it?"

Your team considers your idea. The problems seem surmountable.

Then someone hands you a granola bar. Another person on the team takes out bug spray and binoculars from their pack.

"Let's do this together," you say, taking a bite of your snack. You and your team continue on.

Hugo Duminil-Copin, the 2022 Fields Medal winner, who is the son of a middle-school sports teacher, sees math as a team sport. Once, when Hugo and a friend solved a difficult proof (a way to show that an idea in math is true), they were so excited, they jumped into each other's arms, just like a baseball team does when they win a big game. Hugo has said, "It's much more enjoyable when I share it with somebody." He knows that working together helps you solve problems more easily and is a part of the fun of math.

The Italian mathematician Alessio Figalli worked on the math that describes how clouds move from one shape to another. It was something new that no one had solved … and he didn't do it alone. Alessio collaborates with people all over the world. When he works with others, they sometimes share a chalkboard, writing and talking excitedly. Then they think to themselves silently. Then they go back to the chalkboard. Mathematicians can work with others to figure out which ideas don't work so they can figure out which ones do.

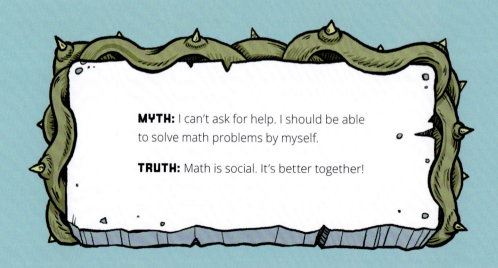

MYTH: I can't ask for help. I should be able to solve math problems by myself.

TRUTH: Math is social. It's better together!

SOPHIE GERMAIN
Born: April 1, 1776, France

"The human spirit requires more resources inside when outside it has less."

Sophie Germain wanted to study math ever since she read about the ancient Greek mathematician Archimedes. But only men were allowed to go to university.

Sophie would have to be creative.

So she used the alias Monsieur Le Blanc, the name of a student at École Polytechnique who had dropped out (without telling the university). Sophie picked up his assignments, worked on the math problems at home and then submitted them using his name. For a while, Sophie studied this way on her own. But soon her professor became curious. He wanted to meet Monsieur Le Blanc, who had improved in math so quickly

The professor was startled to meet Sophie, but he soon became her mentor. They worked on unproven math problems together.

Sophie also used her Monsieur Le Blanc alias to write letters to Carl Friedrich Gauss, one of the most famous mathematicians of all time. They collaborated for years through letters.

When Napoleon's army invaded Prussia, they marched through the town where Carl lived. Sophie arranged for a soldier to travel 200 miles (320 kilometers) to the mathematician's house. The soldier explained he was there to rescue Carl and that Sophie had sent him.

Perplexed, Carl asked, "Who's Sophie?"

When this news reached Sophie in Paris, she wrote a letter to Carl revealing her true identity. He wrote back, impressed at her courage to pursue math when society made it so hard for women.

She became the first woman to win a gold medal from the French Academy of Sciences. (Many years later, in 2003, the Academy launched the Sophie Germain Prize.)

Although Sophie's education was limited because she was a woman, she was creative and able to connect with others to become part of a math community.

RESEARCH SAYS

Asking for Help Helps

Economists analyze information about people's lives and recommend ways to improve their education, health and more. The economists Esther Duflo, Abhijit Banerjee and Michael Kremer looked at small changes that have a big impact in low-income countries. Their work in Kenya and India, for which they won the Nobel Prize in Economic Sciences, showed that when students receive tutoring — especially from older students — they do way better in school.

The benefits of tutoring have been studied around the world. At the University of California, Berkeley, Professor Uri Treisman noticed that a lot of first-year calculus students were dropping out. He wanted to know why some students failed while others excelled. After tracking his students, Uri noticed something: The students who dropped out practiced math alone. The top students in his class worked together in study groups. Could working alone versus working with others make such a big difference? He decided to test that theory.

The university created collaborative workshops for calculus students to learn and study together. Amazingly, the dropout rate completely changed. Not only did students get higher marks, but they also persevered — and stayed in the course.

Why would study groups make a difference?

One reason, he thought, was that seeing others confused by math problems and making mistakes allowed everyone to be similarly vulnerable. It's no big deal to ask for help when others are doing the same.

This sounds obvious, but it's worth pointing out: When you study math with a group, there is a greater chance of one person understanding the problem than if you were to study alone. That person can explain the problem to the others. Students can learn from other students.

These studies, involving different groups of people living very different lives across the ocean from each other, had the same results. Working together is key to success.

Plus, working with others makes learning more fun! Math is better together!

MIND OVER MATH

You Might Not Understand at First. That's Okay.

The first time you look at a new idea in math class, it's like a foggy day. You don't know what you're looking at. You're confused. It feels like you'll never understand it.

But the next time you look at the same idea, the fog lifts a bit and you understand one part of it. But what about the other parts? How do you get from here to there? You don't quite know what you're seeing.

You watch a YouTube video that explains the idea. You ask others what they think. Then you look at it again, and this time you think you see how things connect.

That's what it feels like to learn something new in math. The more you look at it and work on it, the clearer your understanding becomes.

You might find that others are stuck, too. Or maybe someone can show you a new way to see it. By working through the problem together, the fog will lift.

Looking at the same problem repeatedly but in different ways helps you learn.

The next time you see a similar problem, it's clear skies as you get it right away. You hardly remember why you were ever confused!

In math class, ask your teacher if you can work with a partner or in a small group. Ask for help. If you understand something that your classmates do not, try explaining it to them — you will gain a much deeper understanding when you teach it to others. Working together, everyone gets better!

Numbers

What exactly is a number?

We see two apples and use the number 2.

Numbers are an invention. The oldest system of counting is the tally mark. Following that, civilizations around the world — including the ancient Greeks, Egyptians, Romans, Indians, Chinese and Olmecs (from what is now south-central Mexico) — began inventing new ways to count and represent quantities. Through sharing ideas, continually improving on what was known and being curious about what wasn't yet known, the numbers 0, 1, 2, 3, 4, 5, 6, 7, 8, 9 were invented. Using these 10 digits, we can make any number. These numbers are universal. Knowing place value, we see the number 537 and know that it represents five hundreds, three tens and seven ones. We can make negative numbers. We can make fractions. The possibilities are infinite. Having a common language to share ideas helps us spread ideas quickly and easily.

HOW CAN THIS STORY HELP YOU WITH MATH?

The number system spread because mathematicians shared their ideas (way back before the internet — or even the printing press). An important idea in this story is that mathematicians invent and collaborate.

In math class, ask your teacher if you can push your desk beside your friends' desks and work on math problems as a team. Everyone can share how they got to an answer. Math is social. Listen to your classmates and watch how they work out problems. Ask yourself this question: What do they do that could help me? What do I know that might help them? You will get better results when you share your knowledge and build on what others know.

MYTH: If I don't understand a math concept the first time I try to solve it, I never will.

TRUTH: Math can often be confusing when you start to learn a new concept. It's only after seeing it again and again, and in different ways, that it becomes clear. So don't fret if you don't understand things right away. Keep going!

MULTIPLY YOUR POTENTIAL

Lean Back and Look Again

In math class, you will be asked to solve challenging problems. Here is a tip from the researchers Manoj Thomas and Claire Tsai: If you physically move closer to a problem (for example, sit closer to the computer screen), the problem will seem more difficult. But if you lean back, or take a step back, the problem will seem easier.

If a problem is written on a flip chart or on the board, take a step backward and look again.

This helps you in life, too. Ethan Kross, author of the book *Chatter*, has recommended zooming out. When you look at the big picture, you can observe the problem you're facing with a fresh perspective. Ethan wrote that when ninth grade students were told to think about "big-picture reasons for doing schoolwork — for instance, emphasizing how doing well in school would help them land their desired jobs and contribute to society as adults — led them to earn higher GPAs and stay more focused on boring but important tasks." Getting some distance can give you a better view.

It's okay if you don't understand at first. Look again. Ask for help. You don't need to do it alone.

SHOW YOUR WORK

Around the world, there are different words for numbers. For example, in Chinese, the number 90 is 九十 (or *Jiǔ shí*), which translates to "9 tens." This looks like 9 × 10 = 90.

In French, the number 90 is *quatre-vingt-dix*, which translates to "four-twenty-ten." This looks like 4 × 20 + 10 = 90.

1. Write out a few number words in the languages that you speak. What do you notice? Do you see any patterns?
2. Ask someone who speaks another language to share how number words are written in their language. What is similar or different?
3. Did you know that square numbers can be shown as squares? When you multiply a number by itself, you get a square number.
4. Numbers can also have a different meaning. In some cultures, certain numbers are considered lucky or unlucky. Or in sports like baseball or football, the athletes have a number on the back of their jersey. Sometimes, when a player who has made a significant contribution to the sport retires, their number is retired, too. Do you have a favorite number? Why is that number special to you?

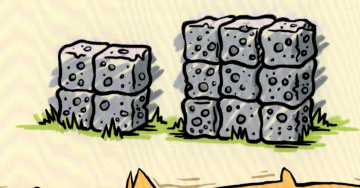

Look at this badge and remember:
When I am stuck on a problem,
then I will ask for help and work
with a partner!

HELPFUL
MISTAKES

You've reached a raging river. After hours in the dense jungle, your team agrees — the rapids are your best chance to find the way home.

The river surges and roars. Only an experienced kayaker could navigate these waters.

Luckily, you and your team *are* experienced. Before leaving on the trip, you prepared for worst-case scenarios.

You swam laps in a pool every morning and took kayaking lessons. In learning how to paddle properly, you made some mistakes — but you made them in the safety of a pool. Then you moved on to practicing on a quiet river, with support staff all along the river's edge. You learned from more of your mistakes. You now know how to use the eddies and how to maneuver to avoid the rocks. You know what to do when you capsize, rolling your hips and using your paddle, to roll upright again. You've practiced many hours together with your team.

You look at each other. You all smile. This is what you've been training for.

"Let's go!"

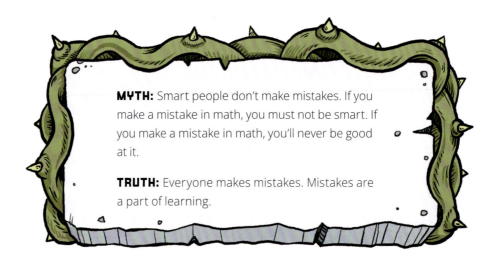

MYTH: Smart people don't make mistakes. If you make a mistake in math, you must not be smart. If you make a mistake in math, you'll never be good at it.

TRUTH: Everyone makes mistakes. Mistakes are a part of learning.

Practice is important. It helps you get better. But when you practice, you'll make mistakes.

Astronauts spend 100 hours training on Earth for every hour in space. Doing things perfectly in space is important. But the way astronauts become good is to make their mistakes on Earth in virtual simulations, which re-create the feeling of being in space.

The National Aeronautics and Space Administration (NASA) headquarters has a huge pool where astronauts practice scuba diving wearing their astronaut suits. This creates the feeling of weightlessness in space. Practicing on Earth allows for precision in space.

Astronauts train like professional athletes would train — constantly! Too often, we see people doing amazing feats without seeing all the practice and all the mistakes they make to become seemingly flawless.

LELAND MELVIN
Born: February 15, 1964, United States

"Nothing is impossible. If you believe in yourself and put your whole heart into whatever you do, you'll be a success."

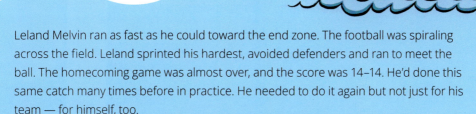

Leland Melvin ran as fast as he could toward the end zone. The football was spiraling across the field. Leland sprinted his hardest, avoided defenders and ran to meet the ball. The homecoming game was almost over, and the score was 14–14. He'd done this same catch many times before in practice. He needed to do it again but not just for his team — for himself, too.

In the stands was a scout from the University of Richmond. Leland was graduating high school, preparing to go to university. This could be a big moment in his life. He reached up, caught the ball … and got the touchdown!

The scout in the crowd offered him a full football scholarship.

At university, Leland worked toward a degree in engineering while also playing football. Upon graduation, he was drafted into the National Football League, the highest level of play for a football player, but an injury cut his athletic career short. Luckily, he had the education — his engineering degree — to apply for a job at NASA.

He got in. Leland would be the first professional football player to go into space.

As an astronaut, Leland practiced using the Canadarm over and over again. The Canadarm is a robotic arm operated by astronauts that can lift huge amounts and needs very little electricity. It has shoulder, elbow and wrist joints and a robotic hand.

In the simulations, Leland operated the controls to manipulate the arm. If the Canadarm swung toward him and crashed into the virtual spacecraft, that was a big mistake! If it had been real life, the astronauts would have had only minutes to get to safety. But it was just a training simulation, a mistake he could learn from.

Astronauts say Earth is a good place to learn and a safe place to make mistakes — in space, though, mistakes are deadly.

Leland practiced many hours to develop his technique and eliminate any errors in his performance. All of that practice paid off. He was chosen to go into space to operate the Canadarm.

Mistakes Grow Your Brain

On the popular education website Youcubed, you'll find videos, posters and the latest brain research telling us that failing is good for our brains. When we make mistakes and persevere through problems, we learn the most. When answers come easily, without struggle, we don't learn as much. The researcher J. S. Moser and his colleagues learned that when people made mistakes, their brains were more active than if they'd got the answer right.

The organizational scientists Nina Keith and Michael Frese showed that an effective way to learn is through what they've called error management training. This means that you pay attention to the mistakes you make. Instead of ignoring mistakes, you watch for them. Then you examine them, talk about them, reflect on them — and learn. The scientists' research supports the idea that taking time to think about your mistakes ("Why do I mess up long division at that step?") helps you get better.

MIND OVER MATH

The Debrief

After a simulation, NASA always debriefs. Astronauts need to listen to feedback about what they did wrong so that they can improve.

Other creative workplaces also debrief. At Pixar, they have a meeting after a movie has been completed. They talk about what didn't work so that they can improve for next time.

In math class, we can reflect, too. This might mean asking yourself, "Why did I answer the question this way? Is there a better approach?"

Or you can talk to your classmates: "Tell me more about why you used that strategy to answer the question."

It's okay to be wrong and for someone to find a mistake with our work. When we make a mistake, we can learn from it, and this will help us understand more deeply.

HISTORY — Measuring Our World

In ancient times, people used parts of their bodies as units of measurement. An inch was the width of a thumb. A yard stretched from a person's nose to the end of their outstretched hand. A pace was the distance of two large steps.

But it was easy to make mistakes with these methods. We all have different thumb widths and arm lengths. How much ground we cover in a couple of steps varies from person to person. If a clothes maker ordered two yards of fine silk, he might not receive enough material despite the silk merchant measuring "exactly" two yards based on his nose-to-hand measurement.

Over time, units of measurement were standardized, meaning they were the same no matter who was measuring and where — even in outer space.

How long is a meter? One ten-millionth of the shortest distance between the North Pole and the equator. Then we created a physical object, a platinum rod, a meter long to stay in the archives of the Academy of Sciences in Paris to be used as a standard around the world.

Still, this measurement could be even more precise. Now, we use a laser and measure the distance light travels in a vacuum.

Around the world, standard units help us to measure. There is even an International Committee for Weights and Measures, which makes sure everything is as precise as it should be. Mathematicians constantly monitor their tools and the measurements to look for mistakes and refine their work.

BIG IDEA — HOW CAN THIS STORY HELP YOU WITH MATH?

An important idea in this story is that mathematicians keep improving. To do this, they use reasoning to find correct solutions.

In math class, reasoning helps you figure out the answer, know that you're right and convince others. Ask yourself: How can I prove I have the right answer? What strategies will help me? Should I work systematically, use trial and improvement or logical reasoning, look for patterns or work backward?

The Millennium Bridge Gets a New Name

The Millennium Bridge, a pedestrian suspension bridge crossing the River Thames in London, England, opened in 2000 with much fanfare. But when people walked across the bridge for the first time, it swayed.

The more people that walked across the bridge, the more it swayed.

Bridges weren't supposed to wobble like this!

The engineers closed the bridge and spent two years fixing the wobble. They added dampers, which are like shocks in a mountain bike. On a bridge, dampers provide a force opposite the motion of the walkers. This helps it to feel more stable.

The engineers tested the bridge by having people walk across it. Then they asked more and more volunteers to walk across it at the same time. They measured the bridge as they added more people. They experimented with designs until they knew precisely what adjustments to make to stop the swaying. Still, as Matt Parker wrote in his book *Humble Pi*, even after two decades of stability, it's still known as the "Wobbly Bridge."

The engineers made a mistake and learned from it; fortunately, there weren't any disasters. There have been other bridges built throughout the world where a math error has caused the bridge to collapse, sometimes with deadly consequences. Building safe structures demands precision, as does flying rockets into outer space, designing roller coasters and so much more. Getting the math perfect can be a matter of life and death.

But this is very different from the mistakes we make when we are learning something new. It is okay to make mistakes in math class. Not just okay; it's expected. Mistakes are helpful. Mistakes make you smarter!

You need to practice to get good at anything …

… which is another way of saying you won't be good at it while you're practicing …

… which is another way of saying you will make mistakes.

The flaws in the first design of the Millennium Bridge taught all of those engineers what to look out for and how to resolve it for any future structural designs. Mistakes are your best teacher.

Video Games

Mark Rober, a YouTuber and former NASA engineer, has said that making mistakes is a part of learning. He compared it to playing a video game. Even though you get killed hundreds of times, you still keep trying. You fall down holes, the final boss wins, or you don't go fast enough or get enough points — those are some of the many setbacks you experience in a video game. But you don't get down on yourself for that. In his TEDx Talk, "The Super Mario Effect," Mark said, "No one ever picks up the controller for the first time and then after jumping into a pit thinks, 'I'm so ashamed. That was such a failure,' and they never want to try again." Even though you don't know how to play the first time, by the tenth time, you're anticipating where the coins are and jumping through the air at just the right time. The more you stick with it, the better you'll be able to do it.

Yet when we look at math, too often we try only once to understand a problem and then think we're failures if we don't get it right away. We think we're doomed to never be good. We need to stop setting unrealistic expectations for ourselves in math class.

Mark designed an online coding puzzle to test how we respond when we make a mistake. He made two versions of the puzzle. In one version, if kids tried the code and it didn't work, the message read, "Please try again. Lose 5 points." These kids tried about five times before giving up. Only half of them solved the puzzle. But in the other version, there was no penalty for mistakes. No one lost points. This group of kids attempted to solve the code about twelve times — way more than the other group. And these additional attempts had a big payoff. Almost 70 percent of the kids solved the puzzle!

When we are penalized for mistakes, we give up more quickly, and many of us never solve the puzzle. But if we are allowed to make mistakes without penalty, we make more attempts, we learn more, and we often solve the puzzle.

MULTIPLY YOUR POTENTIAL

See It. Achieve It.

You'll probably have more tests in math than in any other subject. So here are some tips to help you do better.

The astronaut Chris Hadfield has said, "I picture the most demanding challenge; I visualize what I would need to know how to do to meet it; then I practice until I reach a level of competence where I'm comfortable that I'll be able to perform." You can practice math until you feel ready.

Leland Melvin's football coach helped him mentally prepare for big games. He'd tell him to vividly imagine a football game and then make the game-winning catch. Before a math test, visualize yourself sitting down, reading the questions, enjoying thinking about the problems and writing down your answers.

Another tip comes from Amy Cuddy, a professor at Harvard. In her book *Presence*, she described a study where students wrote about a core value before their university exams. They wrote about what was important to them, such as "Family is important to me" or "I value being creative." Students who practiced self-affirmation and reminded themselves of their most valued strengths were protected from the stress of exams according to the researchers Geoffrey Cohen and David Sherman.

One more test-taking tip — tell yourself you're excited! In Adam Grant's book *Originals*, he wrote about Professor Alison Wood Brooks at Harvard Business School, who asked students to tell themselves they were excited before a math test. These students scored 22 percent higher than those who told themselves to remain calm.

SHOW YOUR WORK

There is an expression that practice makes progress. Choose one of the topics below and reflect on the mistakes you learned from and the practice that went into getting good at something:

1. Do you play a sport? How did practice prepare you?
2. Do you play an instrument? How long do you work on each song? What strategies do you use to learn a new song? How do you know that you play a song well enough? Who gives you feedback?
3. Write about learning something new. (For example, did you learn how to skate, ride a bike, swim, do a cartwheel, program some code or solve the Rubik's Cube?) Do you remember what it felt like not knowing how to do it? How did you improve?
4. Write about something you're really good at. It can be anything at all. Did you know how to do it immediately? If not, how did you master it?

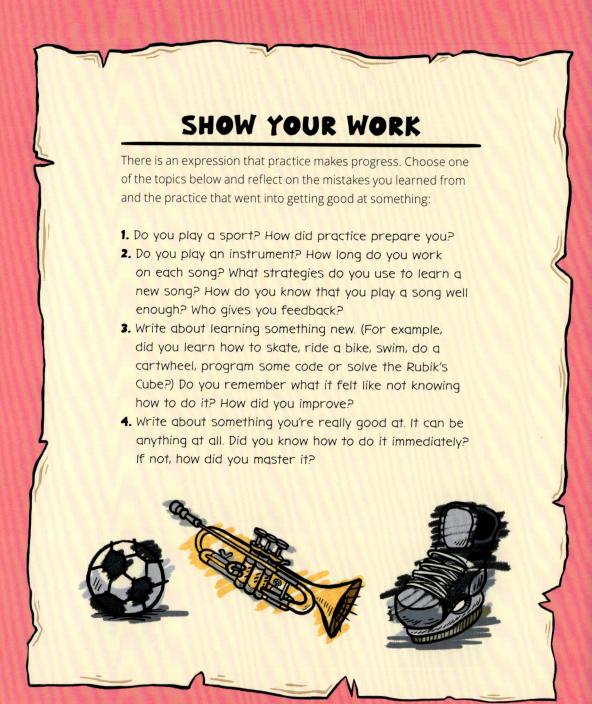

Look at this badge and remember:
When I make a mistake, **then** I will say,
"This mistake will help me get better!"

CREATE IT!

In front of you is a sheer cliff — another obstacle! You'll need to find a way over it to make it out of the jungle. But you and your team can't agree on how to do it.

You decide to split into four smaller groups. One group scales the cliff, planning to go up and over. Another group searches for a high place to launch a glider, wanting to fly over the cliff. Another plans to ride elephants in search of a route to the other side. Your group enters a cave, hoping to find a way through the cliff.

You turn on your headlamp and walk through, its beam slicing through the pitch black. You walk deeper and deeper into the cave. It's damp and cold.

As you move through the cave, you record your route. One person measures the angles with an inclinometer; another uses a measuring tape. You sketch pictures of the cave's interior from all angles. According to your compass, you're heading in the right direction.

After a time, you and your team emerge from the cave — you've made it to the other side! Not long after, the other groups join you. Their routes worked, too! You show them your notebook and explain how you found your way. They share their notes as well.

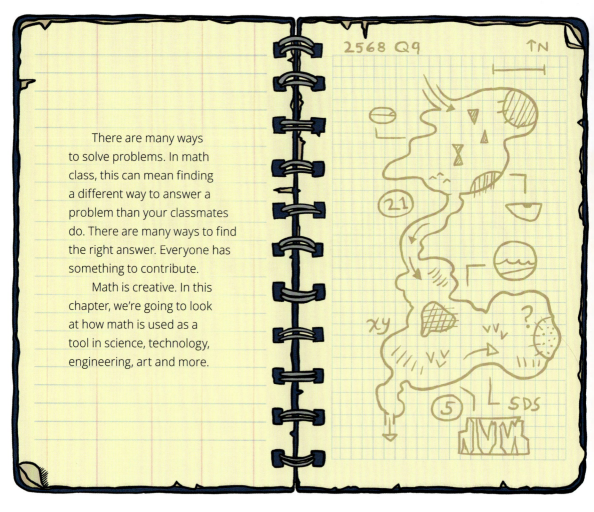

There are many ways to solve problems. In math class, this can mean finding a different way to answer a problem than your classmates do. There are many ways to find the right answer. Everyone has something to contribute.

Math is creative. In this chapter, we're going to look at how math is used as a tool in science, technology, engineering, art and more.

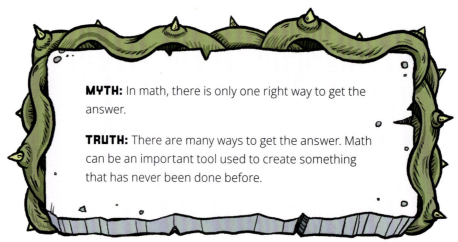

MYTH: In math, there is only one right way to get the answer.

TRUTH: There are many ways to get the answer. Math can be an important tool used to create something that has never been done before.

DAINA TAIMIŅA
Born: August 19, 1954, Latvia

"Mathematics is not scary when you can touch it, think about it in fun ways or, even better — make it yourself."

As a child growing up in Latvia, Daina Taimiņa learned to knit and crochet. She liked to design her own sweaters that were different from her friends'. She earned a PhD in math, but she struggled with hyperbolic geometry. Hyperbolic geometry looks at curving shapes, like a horse's saddle.

Daina later got a job in the math department at Cornell University, where she was asked to teach a course on ... hyperbolic geometry. As a student, Daina had looked at the lines drawn on a flat piece of paper and, like many others, felt confused. Instead of teaching it in the way that she had learned, Daina set out to find a new way to make the subject more understandable.

But how?

In the summer before the course started, Daina sat on the pool deck crocheting as her children splashed in the water. People would walk by and ask her, "What are you making?" likely expecting her to say she was making a scarf or a sweater.

"Oh, I'm crocheting the hyperbolic plane," she would answer.

Using yarn, Daina created a physical model of a hyperbolic plane that students could hold and manipulate. They could see the straight lines, the lines that came close to meeting but then went in infinitely different directions.

The idea went viral!

Her crocheted model was featured in both math magazines and crocheting magazines! It was featured in galleries and museums all over the world, including the Smithsonian.

Daina's skill at crochet helped her visualize an idea in math. Her crochet, a model that students can hold and twist, has helped math students (and teachers) gain a deeper understanding of geometry and has also inspired others to see math as art. There is a common belief that mathematicians work only by scribbling on paper, writing out formulas. The truth is that mathematicians are curious, creative people who use numbers and other tools to understand the world.

RESEARCH SAYS

Playing with Numbers

Jo Boaler, a Stanford math professor, believes everyone can learn math to a high level — and she's got the research to prove it. In her influential article "Fluency Without Fear," Jo and her co-authors, Cathy Williams and Amanda Confer, said that instead of stressing about memorizing math facts, students should play with numbers. Being great at math begins with the idea of number sense.

Number sense helps you to answer the problem of, let's say, 18 × 5. Students who play with numbers might break the problem into smaller chunks, like 10 × 5 and 8 × 5, and then add them together. They might see many different paths to solving the problem. How many ways can you solve 18 × 5?

Jo wrote in a blog post, "I love numbers. One of the things I most love about them is the interesting ways they are made and the ways they combine together to reveal fascinating and seemingly endless patterns."

Using a number line is another way to improve number sense. The researchers Robert Siegler and Geetha Ramani wrote that when preschool students spent fifteen minutes a day playing games using a number line, their number fluency improved enormously, and it took *only four days*! A game with a number line might be something like Chutes and Ladders.

Try to picture what you're calculating. Draw what you see. You can use objects, like base ten blocks, connecting cubes or 3D shapes — even crochet structures — to more deeply understand ideas.

MIND OVER MATH

Use Your Tools

You can work on number fluency by using your fingers.

Some people might think that counting on your fingers is babyish. That's wrong! Math doesn't only need to be done in your head. Using your fingers is a wonderful way to help you see the math.

Researchers say that it's very important for students to count on their fingers. It helps brain development in mathematics. Use your fingers, picture them and think about them. The researcher Brian Butterworth said we need to use our fingers to learn about numbers so that numbers can be represented in our brain.

Your fingers are a useful tool. When you have to add or subtract small numbers, using your hand can help you quickly and easily. When you have to add groups, or skip count for multiplication, using your fingers can help you keep track of how many you've done.

Using your fingers will help you answer the problem in math class, *and* it will help you become fluent with numbers. Win-win!

Humans like math (even if we don't always know it). We like symmetry and patterns and geometric designs. Math is a tool that we use in life to build and create — and enjoy.

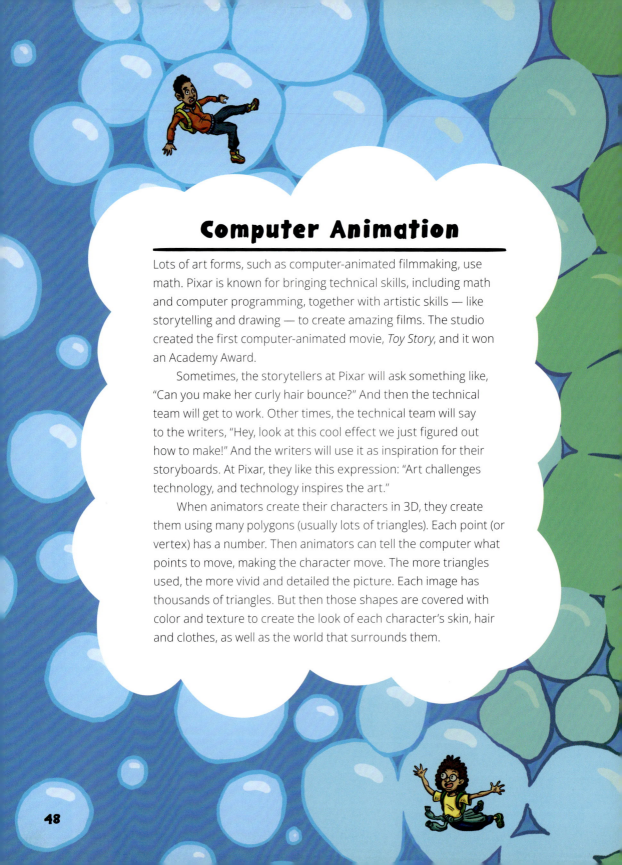

Computer Animation

Lots of art forms, such as computer-animated filmmaking, use math. Pixar is known for bringing technical skills, including math and computer programming, together with artistic skills — like storytelling and drawing — to create amazing films. The studio created the first computer-animated movie, *Toy Story*, and it won an Academy Award.

Sometimes, the storytellers at Pixar will ask something like, "Can you make her curly hair bounce?" And then the technical team will get to work. Other times, the technical team will say to the writers, "Hey, look at this cool effect we just figured out how to make!" And the writers will use it as inspiration for their storyboards. At Pixar, they like this expression: "Art challenges technology, and technology inspires the art."

When animators create their characters in 3D, they create them using many polygons (usually lots of triangles). Each point (or vertex) has a number. Then animators can tell the computer what points to move, making the character move. The more triangles used, the more vivid and detailed the picture. Each image has thousands of triangles. But then those shapes are covered with color and texture to create the look of each character's skin, hair and clothes, as well as the world that surrounds them.

There are a lot of different types of animation jobs at Pixar. For each frame, someone adds lighting, another person adds fur and clothing, and then comes the addition of texture, shading and color — and for each, there is a lot of math involved!

We can learn more in the Khan Academy lessons called "Pixar in a Box." In the lesson about patterns, Ana and Beth talk about their work as shading artists at Pixar. To create believable dinosaur skin in the movie *The Good Dinosaur*, they started by looking at the patterns in a plant called a *Titanopsis*. Then they created a geometric design for the dinosaur's scales, fitting the pieces together like a puzzle. To create scales, they wanted a random pattern, like spots on a giraffe, so they used something called a Voronoi diagram. Then, to add color, they created a computer code so that the larger scales would be one color and the smaller scales would be a different color. The colors were coded to match the size of each scale. This saved them from having to color each scale individually.

Pixar's co-founder, Ed Catmull, has a PhD in computer science, and in 2019 he won the Turing Award for his work bringing computer animation to movies. He's also made creative decisions and considered art and design every day at his job. He's won multiple Academy Awards, the highest honor for creative arts in motion pictures.

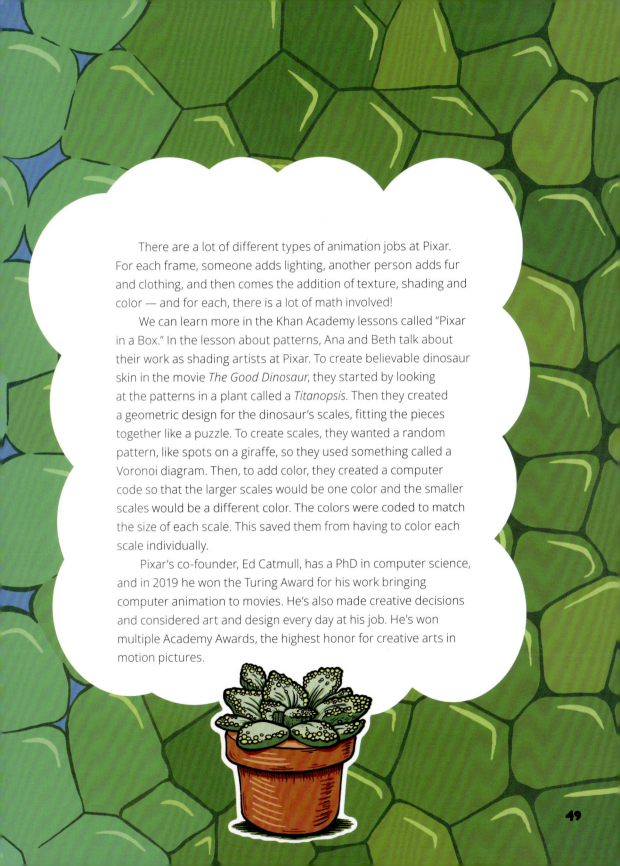

HISTORY: Math and Art Together

Early cultures used shapes and patterns to create beautiful art. Math is still used in many different art forms today.

The *tangram* is a set of shapes that can be rearranged to make different pictures. In Chinese, it's called "seven boards of skill" or "seven ingenious plans."

Origami comes from the Japanese words for "fold" and "paper." If you unfold an origami crane, you will see it's full of shapes and angles! Did you know that people who design airbags in cars consult with origami artists on how to fold the material so that airbags will unfold smoothly? Origami artists also help design satellites that go into space.

Skate parks are community hubs where kids can hang out and develop their skate skills. But to design a geometric skate park, to get the angles just right, the curves perfect and the shapes fitting together like they do, an engineer uses math to make the design work. Skateboarders then flip, spin, jump and ride the angles.

Indigenous beadwork designs use math. Justine Woods is a designer from the Georgian Bay Métis Community who uses beaded patterns to make beautiful art. You can watch her create moccasins on YouTube for the Bata Shoe Museum.

Fashion incorporates math. Diarra Bousso is a fashion designer who brings her love of math, fashion and Senegal together. She designs mathematical patterns and showcases them on Instagram, where people vote for their favorite. In her geometry class, she has students design coloring book pages. Her love of math is a part of the art she creates.

BIG IDEA

HOW CAN THIS STORY HELP YOU WITH MATH?

Math is sometimes described as the science of patterns. An important idea in this story is that mathematicians find new ways to use math to solve problems — they are resourceful.

In math class, look for patterns. Is there a rule that tells you how the pattern repeats, grows or shrinks in a regular way? How can you visualize this problem? Math is everywhere and in everything.

Math is creative, artistic and visual, and there are many ways to do it!

Impossible Art

M. C. Escher's art makes mathematically impossible things look real. In one of his prints, ants travel up and over and around an infinity symbol.

He inspired the father and son mathematicians Lionel and Roger Penrose, who created a design of a staircase that looks like it's going up and going down at the same time. They also created the Penrose triangle, which looks like a two-dimensional drawing of a three-dimensional triangle, but no three-dimensional object could actually be built that way. Roger also came up with Penrose tiling, which uses only two shapes that fit together without any gaps and without repetition — they go together infinitely. It's like putting together a puzzle with only two shapes. You start in the center and fan outward, adding one piece or the other. These designs can be found in art and on floor coverings. Once, a design was also found patterned onto toilet paper, but Roger sued the makers — the company hadn't been given permission to use it!

Penrose tiling is more than art (or math for the fun of it). Close to twenty years after it was invented, it was used to describe quasicrystals (structures in iron and nickel). Math and art together helped us understand chemistry.

Recently, mathematicians have discovered another shape they call "the hat." With only this one shape, you can completely cover a surface, infinitely, without a repeating pattern. This shape was first discovered by a man named David Smith; he wasn't a mathematician, but he did math as a hobby, playing with shapes and doing puzzles. When David discovered "the hat," he reached out to mathematicians to see if he truly had found a new shape. Excitement over this new shape has quilters quilting and bakers making cookie cutters in the same shape. But unlike Penrose tiling, this one isn't patented. If people want to print it on toilet paper — they can!

Will this shape lead to discoveries in physics? Chemistry? Or another field?

Knot Puzzles

Knot puzzles are challenges that mathematicians work on just for fun. Then, often, they later realize that the math they figured out has real-life applications. Think of a hair elastic that's been knotted different ways. Mathematicians have worked on these puzzles over many years. But then mathematicians began using knot theory in other fields. For example, William Thurston connected knot theory to hyperbolic geometry. Vaughan Jones's and Edward Witten's work led to a connection between knot theory and quantum field theory. Knot theory has also helped deepen our understanding in physics, biology and chemistry.

MULTIPLY YOUR POTENTIAL

Words Matter, Even in Math!

The persuasion expert Robert Cialdini has said catchphrases can help you put in more effort. When teachers put up the words *win*, *attain*, *succeed* or *master* on a classroom wall, students did better on a task. Not only did their performance go up but so did their perseverance. These words doubled their motivation to keep going.

Try putting a catchphrase on your wall. It might give you that boost of confidence you need to keep trying.

SHOW YOUR WORK

Reflecting on this chapter, let's look at some of the ways math and art come together. Try one of these activities and then write about your experience:

1. Search up origami instructions. Once you finish a piece, unfold your design and look at the shapes on the paper. What do you notice?
2. Create your own pattern for a quilt square or friendship bracelet.
3. Create your own coloring page using geometric designs.
4. Create a pattern using only "the hat."
5. Try an activity from Khan Academy's "Pixar in a Box" and bring together math, science, computer science and storytelling. Find the activities at www.khanacademy.org/computing/pixar.

Look at this badge and remember: **When** I work on a math problem, **then** I will use creative ways to solve it, such as pictures or unexpected materials to help me visualize the problem.

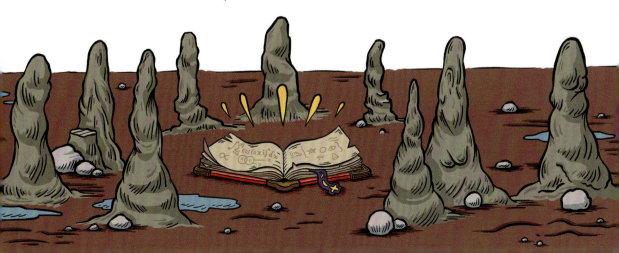

BULLET HOLES AND PIE CHARTS

You're still in the jungle! You feel like you've been struggling for ages, and you're somehow more lost now than when you started.

You want to roar like a jungle cat. You want to rage like a jungle storm. A jungle sloth will get out of the jungle before you do!

But then you take a breath. Okay. Perhaps you were being overly dramatic a second ago.

During your time in the jungle, you *have* gathered information — a lot of it. You've actually come a long way.

Your team takes a look at all the data you've collected since you started. You look at the direction the river flows, the height of the cliffs, the shapes of the caves, the types of vegetation and the animals and insects you've encountered.

You gasp.

It's suddenly clear. Using the data, you can see where to go next. You clearly see the path you've been on and where it leads. You see something you've never seen before. You and your team have found the way out!

And it's not just a path out of *this* jungle. Using what you've learned, it's like you have a magic wand that can whisk you out of *any* jungle at any time!

Now that you're out of the jungle, you can't wait to share your discovery with the world!

This is what it can feel like when you make a discovery in math. You see things you didn't know were there. That's why analyzing data is all about seeing patterns and making connections.

In this chapter, we're going to look at how data can improve our lives.

Back in the mid-1800s, cholera outbreaks were a huge problem in London, England. Cholera spread quickly and killed many people. The disease causes vomiting and diarrhea, which lead to dehydration. But at that time, no one knew how people got sick with cholera. Many thought it was something in the air. A doctor, John Snow, didn't think so. He thought it was spread because of something you ate or drank. To prove it, he did something that had never been done before.

During an 1854 outbreak, he got out a map of London and put dots on the map where the sick people lived. He noticed something compelling. The dots weren't spaced out evenly all over London. Instead, all the people who were sick lived near the Broad Street water pump. Authorities looked at his map and immediately closed the pump. The cholera outbreak stopped. We now know that the disease is caused by contaminated water or food.

Mapping data is an important and visual way to see problems.

MYTH: I don't need to learn math; I can just use a calculator.

TRUTH: Math is more than calculations. Doing math means thinking analytically to solve problems and showing numbers visually. Math can lead you to find the cure for diseases, win games and much more.

TIM CHARTIER
Born: 1969, United States

"Mime makes the invisible quality of math visible."

Tim Chartier is the creator of *Mime-matics*, a show that combines mime and math. In one show, Tim demonstrated infinity by miming an imaginary, infinitely long rope. Using mime, Tim has found a visually captivating way to share math ideas to a wide audience.

He's a math and computer science professor at Davidson College, but he's also a big part of the success of the college basketball team. It all started when three of his math students wanted to help the men's basketball team win more games by providing them with statistics and analytics on their best and weakest plays and positions.

The mathematicians started sitting on the sidelines during games and recording information. Tim wrote, "We charted shots, recording position, shooter and point value."

The math team created a heat map to show from where players took shots. Coaches could make decisions about their lineup — which players worked well together and which players they'd choose to have on the court during the game. The mathematicians also collected data about the players on opposing teams; the coaches could then plan which Davidson player could best handle each opponent.

Tim's math team works with the NBA, NFL, NASCAR and the Olympic and Paralympic Committee. Their sports analytics team eventually grew to 100 mathematicians.

Math helps us visualize what we couldn't before.

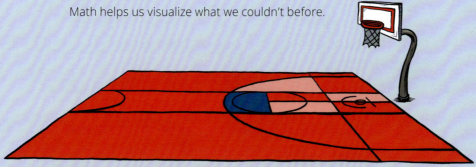

A Room Full of Toilets

Half of the people living around the world don't have access to toilets. Low-income countries don't have money to add plumbing to houses and build sewage treatment systems. This leads to a big problem — contaminated water. People bathe and gather water to cook and wash with from rivers that have human waste floating in them. This makes the people sick.

Data collected by the Institute for Health Metrics and Evaluation revealed that in communities without toilets, poor sanitation is the leading cause of illness and death.

In 2011, there was a two-day Reinvent the Toilet Challenge. Top universities and companies around the world competed to win a grant. The teams needed to create a toilet that uses no plumbing or electricity, costs only pennies a day to operate and is so appealing that everyone would want to use it! Some toilets had solar panels. Some toilets made fertilizer. Some toilets actually made electricity from the poop. Some, if you can believe it, reused the waste to make drinking water!

The creative and lifesaving task of engineering an off-the-grid toilet came from science. But *finding the problem* came from analyzing the numbers.

Statistics is a type of math that gathers large amounts of information. It is the science of collecting information, figuring out what those numbers are showing and then sharing the data with others. It's about using data to make and measure improvements.

Bullet Holes

During World War II, mathematicians working for the U.S. Armed Forces examined planes that returned home from fighting. They noted where all the bullet holes were located.

Some sections of the planes had multiple bullet holes. Other parts of the planes had almost none. In his book *How Not to Be Wrong*, Jordan Ellenberg wrote of the military's challenge: they wanted to make the planes stronger without making them too heavy to fly.

It was clear from looking at the data that some parts of the planes were hit the most. Should they make these areas stronger? Many thought yes. But one man said no.

Abraham Wald looked at the problem differently. He reasoned that if a plane returned home with lots of bullet holes, it showed that these areas could be hit quite often without wrecking the plane. These planes and their pilots made it home safely. These areas didn't need to be reinforced. He wanted to reinforce parts of the plane with no bullet holes.

Hardly any planes returned home with bullet holes over the engine. Abraham suggested this meant that one hit to the engine would crash the plane. But no one could count bullet holes on planes that didn't come back. The designers reinforced the engine area, and more planes returned from battle. Lives were saved.

It's easy to see the bullet holes on the planes that survived, overlooking the ones on the planes that didn't. This is called survivorship bias; that means we count what we see but miss what we don't see.

One of the most important things you can learn in math class is to think like a mathematician. Mathematicians need to be curious, collaborative, resilient and resourceful.

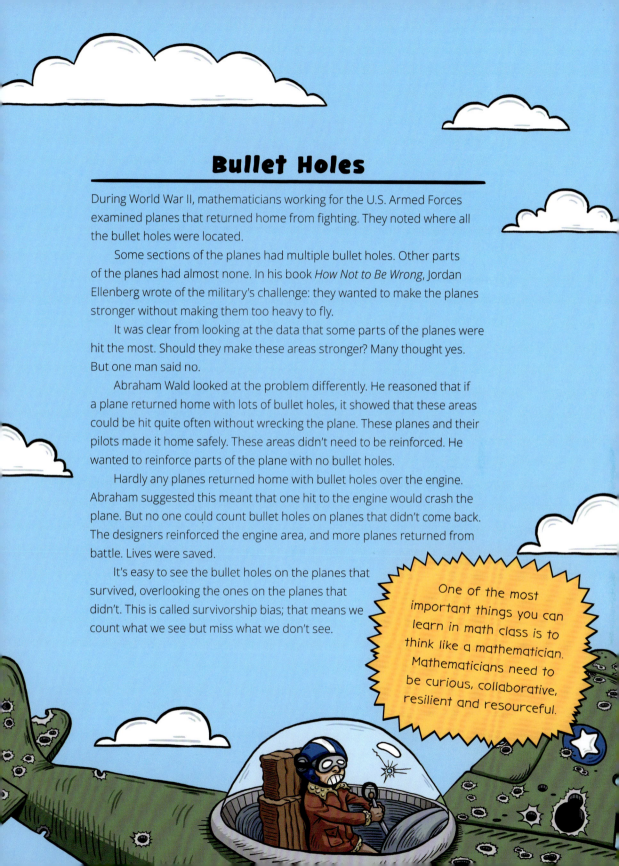

Refresh to Refocus

In Daniel Pink's book *When*, he cited a study by researcher Nolan Pope, who looked at test scores of two million students in Los Angeles and found that students who had math class the first two periods of the day scored higher on tests than the students who had math class the last two periods of the day. Another group of researchers, Hans Henrik Sievertsen, Francesca Gino and Marco Piovesan, looked at students' standardized test scores over four years in Denmark. They saw that students who took the test earlier in the day did much better than those who took the same test later in the day. Using data, the researchers found the best time of day to learn math, and do analytical thinking, was the morning.

Similarly, Daniel pointed to research on the importance of taking an outdoor break. When you're stuck on a problem, leave it. Come back to it later. Sometimes the best way to stay focused and do your best work is to go out for recess!

Consider taking a break from schoolwork by joining a team or club. Angela Duckworth wrote in her book *Grit* that kids who do activities not related to school, like piano lessons or joining a baseball team, "earn better grades, have higher self-esteem, are less likely to get in trouble" and more! Choose something that you like to do and want to learn to be better at.

Doing math in the morning, taking a break outdoors and doing extracurricular activities are all small but important ways to improve your focus.

MIND OVER MATH

When ... Then ...

As mentioned in chapter 1, Peter M. Gollwitzer has been researching how we can make changes in our behavior. He asked students to say either sentence 1 or sentence 2 to themselves as they answered difficult math questions:

1. "I will correctly solve as many problems as possible! And I will tell myself, 'I can do this.'"
2. "I will correctly solve as many problems as possible! And when I start a new problem, then I will tell myself, 'I can do this.'"

The students who said the second sentence solved 15 percent more questions! The second statement is an *action* statement. It tells you when to act. These statements don't work 100 percent of the time. But, through tracking data, researchers have found that using **when/then** statements will give you a higher chance of reaching your goals. Use this research to your advantage!

Make a plan for yourself: **When** *(insert something that you do),* **then** *(insert something that you* will *do).*

HISTORY

Think Like a Mathematician

During the Crimean War, in 1854, Florence Nightingale, along with thirty-eight other nurses, worked at a hospital for wounded soldiers. Conditions were shocking.

The smell of feces and urine filled the air. There was no escaping the lice infestations, and rats weaved between the rows of cots. And the water — well, drinking it could make you deathly sick. Sanitation in the hospitals was so bad that soldiers were more likely to die from diseases they got *while in the hospital* than from their battle wounds! How did they know that? The staff had been recording the reasons why people were dying.

Knowing that soldiers were more likely to die because of unclean conditions in the hospital, Florence and the other nurses made changes. They cleaned the hospital. They even had patients (who were well enough) scrubbing and cleaning. They had volunteers helping with the laundry. All the while, they continued recording the reasons why people were dying. A clean hospital reduced deaths by one-third.

They wanted other hospitals to know about the benefits of cleanliness. To have the biggest impact, Florence wanted to make the numbers easy to understand and memorable, so she used pie charts, which were invented years earlier by William Playfair. Her pie charts worked! Soon after, hospitals around the world began improving their sanitation and saving lives.

Math can help us to see clearly. But we also need to share our results with others. This means finding a way to tell the story behind the numbers.

 **HOW CAN THIS STORY HELP YOU WITH MATH?**

An important idea in this story is that mathematicians communicate and share their ideas. They use numbers, pictures and words to clearly share their results. Numbers in a chart look different when we plot them on a graph. Talking about data helps us see the story the numbers are telling us.

In math class, communicate how you got your answer and why you think it's correct. Ask yourself these questions: How can I show the numbers visually? Could pictures, graphs, pie charts or something else help me share my results?

MULTIPLY YOUR POTENTIAL

Keep It Less than Seven — and Sing It!

The Nobel Prize winner Daniel Kahneman used these research-backed tips when he taught psychology courses:

1. **Seven things or less:** Studies have shown that we can't hold more than seven things in our memory at once. So he taught his students just a few things at a time.
2. **Action songs:** Daniel had his university statistics students sing formulas! He knew the value of singing.

These tips will give you a boost in math class (share them with your teacher!) and in life.

Throughout this book, you've read about many different research studies. All those studies use math. Research is all about asking questions, collecting data, wondering what that data tells us — and then questioning if that data is valid. Researchers collect and analyze lots of data and then make suggestions for how we can best learn and live better.

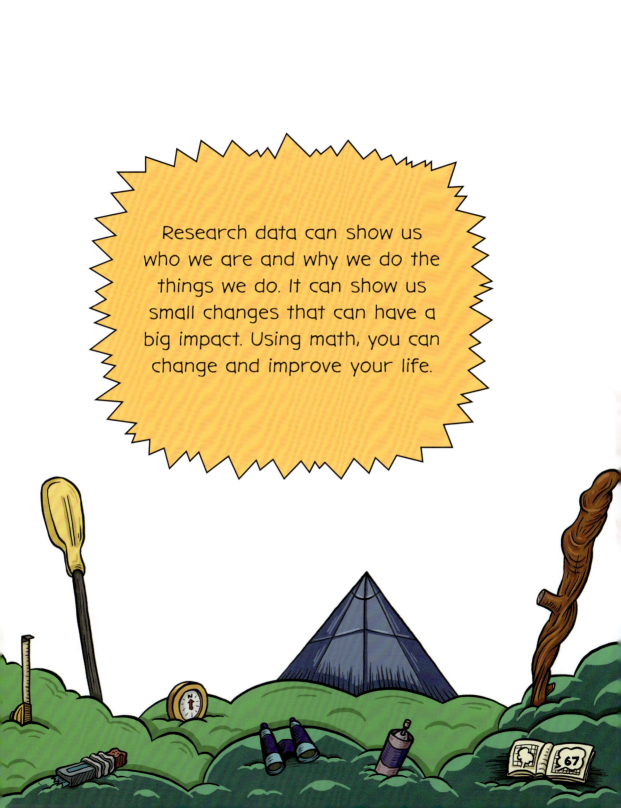

SHOW YOUR WORK

You can use data to help you in your own life. Look at all the things that data can tell you:

1. Track Your Finances

Have you ever needed to save money to buy something you really wanted? Saving money can take time. It's hard to wait. So what do you do?

A good place to start is to track your money — keep data on your spending. That means writing down everything you buy and how much you spend on it. Then look closely at the numbers. Can you find ways to save? Or ways to earn more money?

Looking at numbers can help you to see what you couldn't see before.

2. Your Data Autobiography

Gather some data about your life and create a personal autobiography. What does your life in numbers look like?

What can you include? Here are some ideas: How much time do you spend on your phone or on social media? How many steps do you take? If you take after-school lessons or play a sport, how long do you spend doing them? How many books do you read in a year?

How can you show the numbers in interesting ways?

What do the numbers tell you? Do you see anything you didn't see before?

3. A Pie Chart of Feelings

Make a pie chart about how you feel during the day. How many different emotions did you feel today? How much of your day was spent on each emotion? Here are some feelings you might have felt: happy, joyful, angry, irritated, confused, uncertain, calm, relaxed, sad, upset, stressed, tired, energetic, worried, loved and supported.

What does your pie chart tell you about your day?

Interested in looking at ways to represent data? Check out some of the graphs in the American Statistical Association's "What's Going On in This Graph?" at https://www.amstat.org/whats-going-on-in-this-graph.

Look at this badge and remember: **When** I think math is something I use only in math class, **then** I will remember how math is everywhere, all around me, in art, in buildings — and in the data.

Believe in yourself.
Work hard.
Make mistakes.
Keep going.
Ask for help.
Work with others.
Because it all adds up.

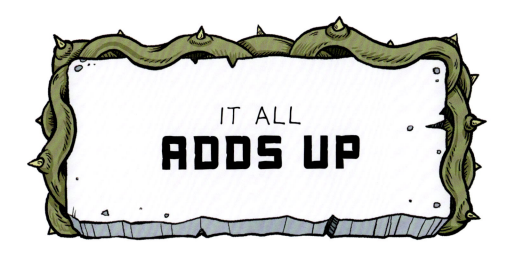

IT ALL ADDS UP

You're not born knowing how to understand math or how to think like mathematicians, but it's something you can learn. One important way you can become better at math is believing in yourself and knowing that you can get better with effort.

Although you can't change how tall you become, you can change your abilities. It all starts with confidence. If you think you can do it, then you'll put in the effort, and you'll keep going. It all adds up.

You have a unique way of seeing the world and looking at problems. Nobel Prize–winning physicist Richard Feynman noticed that even something that we think we all do the same, something as seemingly straightforward as counting, we do differently.

Some people say the numbers in their heads: "One, two, three, four, five ..."

Others might see the numbers go by on a number line, like a long tape measure: 1, 2, 3, 4, 5 ...

Some people see math in colors, like purple, red or blue.

Still others might do something completely different when they count.

This happens all the time in math class. You might get the same answer as your classmates, but the way you got there could be very different.

When you see a math problem, think about it this way: "I have a unique way to solve this problem. I can draw a picture of what this problem looks like, or I can use blocks or a number line. I will take my time. It will feel so good once I discover the answer!"

When you see a challenging math problem, then say,

"I've got this."

Use the ideas in this book to see that there are no limits to what you can learn. You were born a curious learning machine.

You're going to do amazing things!

"Whether you think you can,
or you think you can't,
you are right."

Henry Ford

DEDICATION

To Quinn, Emma, Rosie, Vivienne and my husband, Ed

ACKNOWLEDGMENTS

Thank you to Dr. John Mighton for your insightful suggestions. To Patricia Ocampo, for your vision and thoughtful editing. To Sean Simpson, for your clever illustrations. To Andrew Dupuis, for your art direction and creative design layout. And to the amazing team at Kids Can Press. To Brian Henry, for your guidance. To my parents, Rod and Nancy, for your support. To my children, Quinn, Emma, Rosie and Vivienne, for your enthusiasm. And to my husband, Ed, for reading draft after draft and encouraging me every step of the way. Thank you!

— Carleigh

SOURCES CONSULTED

- Banerjee, Abhijit V., and Esther Duflo. "Why Aren't Children Learning?" *Development Outreach* 13, no. 1 (2011): 36–44. https://openknowledge.worldbank.org/server/api/core/bitstreams/e1dd4683-629c-59c7-9952-4512ce99a04f/content.
- Barcelo, Hélène, and Stephen Kennedy, eds. "Maryam Mirzakhani: 1977–2017." *Notices of the American Mathematical Society* 65, no. 10 (November 2018): 1221–1247. https://www.ams.org/journals/notices/201810/rnoti-p1221.pdf.
- Bell, E. T. *Men of Mathematics: The Lives and Achievements of the Great Mathematicians from Zeno to Poincaré*. Touchstone, 1986.
- Bieleke, Maik, Lucas Keller, Peter M. Gollwitzer. "If-Then Planning. *European Review of Social Psychology* 32, no. 1 (2020): 88-122. https://doi.org/10.1080/10463283.2020.1808936.
- Boaler, Jo. "Anyone Can Learn to High Levels." Youcubed at Stanford University, 2017. https://www.youcubed.org/wp-content/uploads/2017/05/Anyone-Can-Learn-to-High-Levels.pdf.
- Boaler, Jo. "Developing Mathematical Mindsets: The Need to Interact with Numbers Flexibly and Conceptually." *American Educator* 42, no. 4 (Winter 2018 -2019): 28-40. https://files.eric.ed.gov/fulltext/EJ1200568.pdf.
- Boaler, Jo. *Limitless Mind: Learn, Lead, and Live Without Barriers*. HarperOne, 2019.
- Boaler, Jo. *Mathematical Mindsets: Unleashing Students' Potential Through Creative Mathematics, Inspiring Messages and Innovative Teaching*. With a foreword by Carol Dweck. Jossey-Bass, 2015.
- Boaler, Jo, and Lang Chen. "Why Kids Should Use Their Fingers in Math Class." *The Atlantic*. April 13, 2016. https://www.theatlantic.com/education/archive/2016/04/whykids-should-use-their-fingers-in-math-class/478053/.
- Boaler, Jo, Lang Chen, Cathy Williams, and Montserrat Cordero. "Seeing as Understanding: The Importance of Visual Mathematics for our Brain and Learning." https://www.hilarispublisher.com/open-access/seeing-as-understanding-the-importance-of-visual-mathematics-for-our-brain-and-learning-2168-9679-1000325.pdf.
- Boaler, Jo, Cathy Williams and, Amanda Confer. "Fluency Without Fear: Research Evidence on the Best Ways to Learn Math Facts." Youcubed at Stanford University, updated January 28, 2015. https://www.youcubed.org/wp-content/uploads/2017/09/Fluency-Without-Fear-1.28.15.pdf.
- Carey, Bjorn. "Stanford's Maryam Mirzakhani Wins Fields Medal." *Stanford Report*, August 12, 2014. https://news.stanford.edu/stories/2014/08/stanfords-maryam-mirzakhani-wins-fields-medal.
- Cialdini, Robert. *Pre-Suasion: A Revolutionary Way to Influence and Persuade*. Simon and Schuster, 2016.
- Cuddy, Amy. *Presence: Bringing Your Boldest Self to Your Biggest Challenges*. Little Brown Spark, 2015.

- Devlin, Keith. *The Math Gene: How Mathematical Thinking Evolved and Why Numbers Are Like Gossip*. Basic Books, 2000.
- Devlin, Keith. *Mathematics Education for a New Era: Video Games as a Medium for Learning*. CRC Press, 2011.
- Dweck, Carol. *Mindset: The New Psychology of Success*, updated ed. Ballantine Books, 2016.
- Ellenberg, Jordan. *How Not to Be Wrong: The Power of Mathematical Thinking*. Penguin, 2014.
- Feynman, Richard. *Classic Feynman: All the Adventures of a Curious Character*. W. W. Norton, 2005.
- Gollwitzer, Peter M., and Paschal Sheeran, "Implementation Intentions." https://cancercontrol.cancer.gov/sites/default/files/2020-06/goal_intent_attain.pdf.
- Grant, Adam. *Originals: How Non-Conformists Move the World*. Viking, 2016.
- Hammond, Alexander C. R. "Heroes of Progress, Pt. 45, John Snow." Human Progress, May 28, 2020. https://www.humanprogress.org/heroes-of-progress-pt-45-john-snow/.
- Hartnett, Kevin. "A Traveler Who Finds Stability in the Natural World." *Quanta Magazine*, August 1, 2018. https://www.quantamagazine.org/a-traveler-who-findsstability-in-the-natural-world-20180801/.
- Hoffman, Reid, host. *Masters of Scale*. Podcast. Episode 52: "Bill Gates: The Biggest Success Story You Haven't Heard (Part 2)." https://mastersofscale.com/bill-gates-biggest-success-story-youhavent-heard/.
- Khan, Salman. *The One World Schoolhouse: Education Reimagined*. Twelve, 2012.
- Khan Academy. "Pixar in a Box" (course). https://www.khanacademy.org/computing/pixar/.
- Klarreich, Erica. "Hobbyist Finds Math's Elusive 'Einstein' Tile." *Quanta Magazine*, April 4, 2023. https://www.quantamagazine.org/hobbyist-finds-maths-elusive-einsteintile-20230404/.
- Klaareich, Erica. "A Tenacious Explorer of Abstract Surfaces." *Quanta Magazine*, August 12, 2014. https://www.quantamagazine.org/maryam-mirzakhani-is-first-womanfields-medalist-20140812/.
- Leland Melvin's website: https://www.lelandmelvin.com/.
- Lewis, Michael. *The Undoing Project: A Friendship That Changed Our Minds*. Norton, 2017.
- Martin, Steve J., Noah J. Goldstein, and Robert B. Cialdini. *The Small Big: Small Changes that Spark Big Influence*. Grand Central Publishing, 2014.
- Merow, Sophia D. "'Creative Mathematician' Transforms Student Errors into 'Sartorial Celebration.'" *Notices of the American Mathematical Society* 67, no. 6 (June/July 2020): 883–885. https://www.ams.org/journals/notices/202006/rnoti-p883.pdf.
- Mlodinow, Leonard. *Elastic: Unlocking Your Brain's Ability to Embrace Change*. Pantheon Books, 2018.

- Moser, Jason S., Hans S. Schroder, Carrie Heeter, Tim P. Moran, and Yu-Haw Lee. "Mind Your Errors: Evidence for a Neural Mechanism Linking Growth Mind-Set to Adaptive Posterror Adjustments." *Psychological Science* 22, no. 12 (2011): 1484–1489. https://doi.org/10.1177/0956797611419520.
- NRICH Project. "Developing Mathematical Mindsets — Primary Teachers." Millennium Mathematics Project, University of Cambridge. https://nrich.maths.org/12639.
- NRICH Project. "Thinking Mathematically — Secondary Students." Millennium Mathematics Project, University of Cambridge. https://nrich.maths.org/8767.
- Parker, Matt. *Humble Pi: When Math Goes Wrong in the Real World*. Riverhead Books, 2020.
- Pink, Daniel H. *When: The Scientific Secrets of Perfect Timing*. Riverhead Books, 2018.
- Richeson, David S. "Why Mathematicians Study Knots." *Quanta Magazine*, October 31, 2022. https://www.quantamagazine.org/why-mathematicians-study-knots-20221031/.
- Schattschneider, Doris. "The Mathematical Side of M. C. Escher." *Notices of the American Mathematical Society* 57, no. 6 (June/July 2010): 706–718. https://www.ams.org/notices/201006/rtx100600706p.pdf.
- Selanders, Louise. "Florence Nightingale". *Encyclopedia Britannica*, last updated December 21, 2024. https://www.britannica.com/biography/Florence-Nightingale.
- Siegler, Robert S., and Geetha B. Ramani. "Playing Linear Numerical Board Games Promotes Low-Income Children's Numerical Development." *Developmental Science* 11, no. 5 (2008): 655–611. https://siegler.tc.columbia.edu/wpcontent/uploads/2019/02/siegram08.pdf.
- Steele, Claude M. *Whistling Vivaldi: How Stereotypes Affect Us and What We Can Do*. W. W. Norton, 2010.
- Strogatz, Steven. *Infinite Powers: How Calculus Reveals the Secrets of the Universe*. Houghton Mifflin Harcourt, 2019.
- Taimiņa, Daina. *Crocheting Adventures with Hyperbolic Planes: Tactile Mathematics, Art and Craft for All to Explore*. AK Peters, 2009.

SOURCES CITED

- **p. 5:** Cook, Mariana. *Mathematicians: An Outer View of the Inner World*. Princeton University Press, 2009.
- **p. 8, 12, 22, 27, 32:** Mighton, John. *The Myth of Ability: Nurturing Mathematical Talent in Every Child*. House of Anansi Press, 2003.
- **p. 9:** Beheshti, Roya. "Maryam Mirzakhani in Iran." *Notices of the American Mathematical Society* 65, no 10 (November 2018): 1222–1224. https://www.ams.org/journals/notices/201810/rnoti-p1221.pdf.

- **p. 9:** Bjorn Carey. "Stanford's Maryam Mirzakhani wins Fields Medal." *Stanford Report*, August 12 2014. https://news.stanford.edu/stories/2014/08/stanfords-maryam-mirzakhani-wins-fields-medal.
- **p. 10:** Dweck, Carol. "The Power of Believing That You Can Improve." TEDx Talk, November 2014. https://www.ted.com/talks/carol_dweck_the_power_of_believing_that_you_can_improve.
- **p. 11:** Clear, James. "The Goldilocks Rule: How to Stay Motivated in Life and Business." Jamesclear.com. https://jamesclear.com/goldilocks-rule.
- **p. 12–13:** Mighton, John. *All Things Being Equal: Why Math Is the Key to a Better World*. Alfred A. Knopf Canada, 2020.
- **p. 16:** Ariely, Dan. "What Makes Us Feel Good about Our Work?" TEDx Talk, Buenos Aires, Argentina, October 2012. https://www.ted.com/talks/dan_ariely_what_makes_us_feel_good_about_our_work.
- **p. 17, 35, 48–49:** Catmull, Ed, and Amy Wallace. *Creativity, Inc.: Overcoming the Unseen Forces that Stand in the Way of True Inspiration*. Random House Canada, 2014.
- **p. 22:** Cepelewicz, Jordana. "For His Sporting Approach to Math, a Fields Medal." *Quanta Magazine*, July 5, 2022. https://www.quantamagazine.org/hugo-duminil-copinwinsthefields-medal-20220705/.
- **p. 23:** Bardoe, Cheryl. *Nothing Stopped Sophie: The Story of Unshakable Mathematician Sophie Germain*. Little Brown and Company, 2018.
- **p. 27:** Kross, Ethan. *Chatter: The Voice in Our Head, Why It Matters, and How to Harness It*. Crown, 2021.
- **p. 32–33, 39:** Melvin, Leland. *Chasing Space*, young readers' ed. Amistad, 2017.
- **p. 35, 39:** Hadfield, Chris. *An Astronaut's Guide to Life on Earth*. Random House Canada, 2013.
- **p. 38:** Rober, Mark. "The Super Mario Effect: Tricking Your Brain into Learning More." TEDx Talk, Philadelphia, PA, April 2018. https://www.ted.com/talks/mark_rober_the_super_mario_effect_tricking_your_brain_into_learning_more.
- **p. 45:** Samuels, David. "Knit Theory." *Discover Magazine*, March 6, 2006. https://www.discovermagazine.com/the-sciences/knit-theory.
- **p. 45:** Taimiņa, Daina. "Crocheting Hyperbolic Planes." TEDx Talk, Riga, Latvia, June 2012. https://www.youtube.com/watch?v=w1TBZhd-sN0.
- **p. 46:** Boaler, Jo. "Why I Love Numbers." Joeboaler.org. https://joboaler.org/2022/04/23/why-i-love-numbers/.
- **p. 59:** Chartier, Tim. *Get in the Game: An Interactive Introduction to Sports Analytics*. Illustrated by Ansley Earle. University of Chicago Press, 2022.
- **p. 59:** Young, Robin, host. "An Unusual Way to Teach Math: Miming." *Here & Now*. NPR, December 17, 2013. https://www.npr.org/transcripts/252003824?storyId=252003824.
- **p. 62:** Duckworth, Angela. *Grit: The Power of Passion and Perseverance*. Collins, 2016.

INDEX

Academy Award, 17, 48, 49
affirmations, 39
animators, 17, 48, 49, 50, 52
art and design, 45, 48–49, 52, 54
asking for help, 11, 16, 24, 25
astronauts, 32, 33, 35

behavior, 16, 18, 38, 63

challenges, 11, 16
Chartier, Tim, 59
cholera outbreak, 58
computer animation, 48–49
confidence, 11, 53, 71
creativity, 17, 44, 45, 48, 49, 50
crochet, 45, 46

data
   analyzing, 24, 58, 59, 60, 61, 62, 66
   collecting, 57, 59, 60, 61, 62, 64, 66, 68
   displaying, 58, 59, 64, 68
   sharing, 57, 59, 60, 64, 65

economists, 24
effort, 10, 12, 15, 17, 38, 53, 71
engineering, 37, 50, 60

fashion, 50
Fields Medal, 9, 22
filmmaking, 16, 48–49
focus, 62

games and puzzles, 38, 46, 53
Gauss, Carl Friedrich, 23
geometry, 45, 49, 50
Germain, Sophie, 23
Goldilocks Rule, 11
graphs and pie charts, 64, 65, 68

helpful tips, 27, 39, 66
hyperbolic plane, 45

Indigenous beadwork, 50

JUMP Math, 13

knot theory, 53

learning, 12
   best time for, 62
   something new, 16, 25

math
   as a tool, 44, 47
   in nature, 13, 22
   myths, 8, 22, 27, 32, 44, 58
   tests, 39, 62
Math Olympiad, 9, 11
measurements, 14, 36
Melvin, Leland, 33, 39
Mighton, John, 12–13
Millennium Bridge, 37
mindset, 10, 12–13
Mirzakhani, Miriam, 9, 11
mistakes, 31, 32, 33, 34, 35, 36, 37, 38
money, 68
motivation, 16, 38, 53

NASA, 32, 33, 35
Nightingale, Florence, 64
Nobel Prize, 24, 66, 71
numbers
   counting, 26, 47, 71
   place value, 26
   words for numbers, 28
   fluency, 46
   counting on fingers, 47

origami, 50

patterns, 13, 46, 49, 50, 51, 52, 58
Penrose, 52
perseverance, 10, 12, 15, 24, 34, 38, 53
perspective, 27
Pixar, 17, 35, 48, 49
practice, 11, 16, 17, 31, 32, 33, 37, 40
problem solving, 27, 44

reasoning, 36
research studies, 10, 16, 18, 24, 34, 38, 39, 46, 62, 63, 66
Rober, Mark, 38

sanitation, 60, 64
sharing ideas, 26, 43, 59, 65
skate parks, 50
Snow, John, 58
sports, 22, 28, 33, 39, 59
stargazing, 15
statistics, 59, 60

Taimiņa, Daina, 45
tangram, 50
teamwork, 21, 22, 23, 24, 25, 26, 43
"the hat" shape, 52
time, 14
toilets, 60
Treisman, Uri, 24
tutoring, 12, 24

video games, 38
visualizing, 39, 45, 46, 47, 58, 59

war planes, 78
when/then statements, 18, 19, 29, 41, 55, 63, 69
Wobbly Bridge, 37
women in math, 9, 23, 45, 46, 50

Youcubed, 34

Carleigh Wu is a math coach who has also worked as a teacher and librarian. She lives in Toronto, Ontario, with her husband and four children. Carleigh's favorite thing about numbers is how dependable they are. She can always count on them.

Sean Simpson is a graduate of Sheridan College's illustration program. He is a marketing designer by day and illustrator by night. Check out more of his work at www.seansimpsonillustration.com. Sean lives in Edmonton, Alberta, with his wife and dog.